Pamela
Walks the Dog

By
Christine Marlin

Illustrated by
Hilda van Stockum

BETHLEHEM BOOKS • IGNATIUS PRESS
BATHGATE, N.D.   SAN FRANCISCO

ISBN 1-883937-61-2
Library of Congress Control Number: 2001092580

Cover art by Hilda van Stockum-Marlin
Book and cover design by Davin Carlson

First printing, September 2001

Bethlehem Books • Ignatius Press
10194 Garfield Street South
Bathgate, ND 58216
www.bethlehembooks.com

Printed in Canada on acid free paper

For Jacqueline

Pamela thought that it would be a good time to take the dog for a walk.

So she put on her shoes
and her coat . . .

and she took her favorite drink . . .

and made herself a sandwich
in case she got hungry . . .

and took along a
story to read . . .

and she washed
her hands . . .

and combed her hair . . .

and found a
perfect leash . . .

and she was all set—
but there was one problem—

Pamela did not *have*
a dog!

So she took her little sister instead.

About the Author

Christine Marlin is a writer currently teaching English literature at a university in the United Arab Emirates. She has published articles in newspapers and magazines and served as an editing consultant. She is the oldest daughter of Randal Marlin, oldest son of Hilda van Stockum (known as "Peter" in *The Mitchells: Five for Victory*).

About the Illustrator

Hilda van Stockum, parent of six children and grandparent of more, has written and illustrated numerous books for children. She studied art in Ireland and the Netherlands and is a well-respected still-life artist. Born Dutch, married to an American, she now resides in England.